Blooming
Beneath the Sun

ILLUSTRATOR'S NOTE

It is with the scissors that my mother used in sewing and embroidery
that I, in turn, used in cutting the colored papers for ALL of
the collage compositions in this book. Her hand in mine.

A
atheneum

ATHENEUM BOOKS FOR YOUNG READERS
An imprint of Simon & Schuster Children's Publishing Division
1230 Avenue of the Americas, New York, New York 10020
Illustrations copyright © 2019 by The Ashley Bryan Center, a Maine Corporation
All rights reserved, including the right of reproduction in whole or in part in any form.
ATHENEUM BOOKS FOR YOUNG READERS is a registered trademark of
Simon & Schuster, Inc. Atheneum logo is a trademark of Simon & Schuster, Inc.
For information about special discounts for bulk purchases, please contact Simon & Schuster
Special Sales at 1-866-506-1949 or business@simonandschuster.com.
The Simon & Schuster Speakers Bureau can bring authors to your live event.
For more information or to book an event, contact the Simon & Schuster Speakers Bureau
at 1-866-248-3049 or visit our website at www.simonspeakers.com.
Book design by Vikki Sheatsley · The text for this book was set in Artcraft. · The illustrations for
this book were rendered with Canson construction paper. · Manufactured in China · 0119 SCP
First Edition · 10 9 8 7 6 5 4 3 2 1
CIP data for this book is available from the Library of Congress.
ISBN 978-1-5344-4092-0 · ISBN 978-1-5344-4093-7 (eBook)

Blooming
Beneath the Sun

Poems by CHRISTINA ROSSETTI

Art by ASHLEY BRYAN

A Caitlyn Dlouhy Book

ATHENEUM BOOKS FOR YOUNG READERS

New York   London   Toronto   Sydney   New Delhi

To Grace and Tess Meis,
and my many nieces and nephews

—A. B.

POEMS
INCLUDED

Kookoorookoo! Kookoorookoo!

"Kookoorookoo! kookoorookoo!"

Crows the cock before the morn;

"Kikirikee! kikirikee!"

Roses in the east are born.

"Kookoorookoo! kookoorookoo!"

Early birds begin their singing;

"Kikirikee! kikirikee!"

The day, the day, the day is springing.

Color

What is pink? a rose is pink
By a fountain's brink.
What is red? a poppy's red
In its barley bed.
What is blue? the sky is blue
Where the clouds float thro'.
What is white? a swan is white
Sailing in the light.

What is yellow? pears are yellow,
Rich and ripe and mellow.
What is green? the grass is green,
With small flowers between.
What is violet? clouds are violet
In the summer twilight.
What is orange? Why, an orange,
Just an orange!

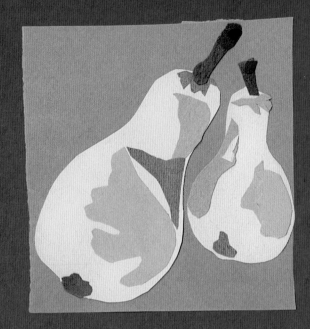

Pussy Has a Whiskered Face

Pussy has a whiskered face,
Kitty has such pretty ways;

Doggie scampers when I call,
And has a heart to love us all.

Who Has Seen the Wind?

Who has seen the wind?
Neither I nor you:
But when the leaves hang trembling,
The wind is passing through.

Who has seen the wind?
Neither you nor I:
But when the trees bow down their heads,
The wind is passing by.

If I Were a Queen

If I were a Queen,
What would I do?
I'd make you King,
And I'd wait on you.

If I were a King,
What would I do?
I'd make you Queen,
For I'd marry you.

Mother Shake the Cherry-Tree

Mother shake the cherry-tree,
Susan catch a cherry;
Oh how funny that will be,
Let's be merry!

One for brother, one for sister,

Two for mother more,

Six for father, hot and tired,

Knocking at the door.

Wrens and Robins in the Hedge

Wrens and robins in the hedge,
Wrens and robins here and there;
Building, perching, pecking, fluttering,
Everywhere!

The wind has such a rainy sound   The sea has such a windy sound, -

Moaning through the town,   Will the ships go down?

The Wind Has Such a Rainy Sound

The apples in the orchard
Tumble from their tree. -

Oh will the ships go down, go down,
In the windy sea?

The Peacock Has a Score of Eyes

The peacock has a score of eyes,
  With which he cannot see;
The cod-fish has a silent sound,
  However that may be;

No dandelions tell the time,
  Although they turn to clocks;
Cat's-cradle does not hold the cat,
  Nor foxglove fit the fox.

I Dreamt I Caught a Little Owl

"I dreamt I caught a little owl
And the bird was blue—"

"But you may hunt for ever
And not find such a one."

"I dreamt I set a sunflower,
And red as blood it grew—"

"But such a sunflower never
Bloomed beneath the sun."

Lie-a-Bed

Lie a-bed,
Sleepy head,
Shut up eyes, bo-peep;
Till daybreak
Never wake: —
Baby, sleep.

Where Innocent Bright-Eyed Daisies Are

Where innocent bright-eyed daisies are,

With blades of grass between,

Each daisy stands up like a star

Out of a sky of green.

If a Pig Wore a Wig

If a pig wore a wig,
What could we say?
Treat him as a gentleman;
And say "Good day."

HURT NO LIVING THING

Hurt no living thing:
Ladybird, not butterfly
Nor moth with dusty wing,
Nor cricket chirping cheerily,
Nor grasshopper so light of leap,
Nor dancing gnat, nor beetle fat,
Nor harmless worms that creep.

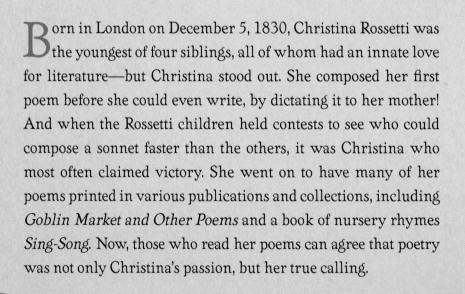

Born in London on December 5, 1830, Christina Rossetti was the youngest of four siblings, all of whom had an innate love for literature—but Christina stood out. She composed her first poem before she could even write, by dictating it to her mother! And when the Rossetti children held contests to see who could compose a sonnet faster than the others, it was Christina who most often claimed victory. She went on to have many of her poems printed in various publications and collections, including *Goblin Market and Other Poems* and a book of nursery rhymes *Sing-Song*. Now, those who read her poems can agree that poetry was not only Christina's passion, but her true calling.